THE WILD CHRISTMAS REINDEER

20TH ANNIVERSARY EDITION

written and illustrated by

Jan Brett

G. P. PUTNAM'S SONS
AN IMPRINT OF PENGUIN GROUP (USA) INC.

To Natalie and Stephanie Larsen

Published simultaneously in Canada. Manufactured in China by RR Donnelley Asia Printing Solutions Ltd.

Airbrush backgrounds by Joseph Hearne. Type design by Gunta Alexander.

Library of Congress Cataloging-in-Publication Data

Brett, Jan, 1949– The wild Christmas reindeer / written and illustrated by Jan Brett.

p. cm. Summary: After a few false starts, Teeka discovers

the best way to get Santa's reindeer ready for Christmas Eve.

[1. Reindeer—Fiction. 2. Christmas—Fiction.] I. Title. PZ7.B7559 Wi 1990 [E]—dc20 89-36095

ISBN 978-0-399-22192-7

25 27 29 30 28 26 24

Anniversary Edition, 2010.

The *Wild Christmas Reindeer* began with thoughts of the North Pole. I had never been there, but as I started wondering about it, I imagined wandering onto a vast snowy landscape. Before I knew it, eight reindeer walked by, leaving footprints in the snow.

Where were they going? Were they Santa's reindeer? My imagination began to soar. What if Santa asked an elf to get the reindeer ready to fly for Christmas? Now I knew I had the story I wanted to tell.

I would call my elf Teeka. A first line popped into my head: "Teeka was excited. And a little afraid." That's how I felt sometimes when I was trying something new. But as I started to write, Teeka took over and became her own person, and the eight reindeer took on personalities of their own.

Before I could begin painting, I knew I needed to meet real reindeer. So my husband, Joe, and I went to Maine to see caribou, the North American variety of the European reindeer. I wanted to touch their fur, tickle their tummies, look at their hooves, feel their antlers. I worried that they would be shy and not let me near them. But when the door to their pen opened, two happy caribou came barreling over and almost knocked us down, nuzzling us and running off with my pom-pom hat. The problem was not getting close to them, but getting far enough away so that Joe could photograph them.

Every Christmas since that time twenty years ago, I think of Teeka and the reindeer. We had so much fun together. I hope you will too.

Merry Christmas!

Jan Brett

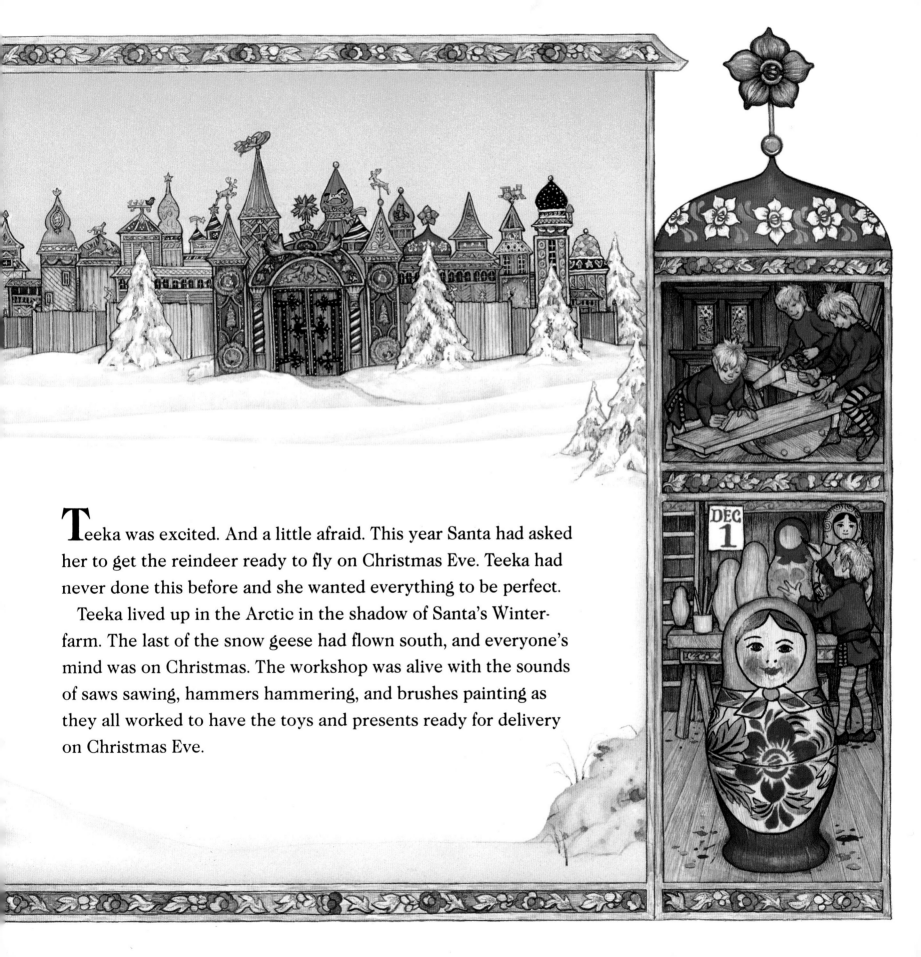

Teeka was excited. And a little afraid. This year Santa had asked her to get the reindeer ready to fly on Christmas Eve. Teeka had never done this before and she wanted everything to be perfect.

Teeka lived up in the Arctic in the shadow of Santa's Winter-farm. The last of the snow geese had flown south, and everyone's mind was on Christmas. The workshop was alive with the sounds of saws sawing, hammers hammering, and brushes painting as they all worked to have the toys and presents ready for delivery on Christmas Eve.

Teeka knew it was time for her to go in search of the reindeer. They had been out on the tundra, wild and free since last Christmas, and Teeka was sure they wouldn't want to go back to Winterfarm to train. She would have to be strong and firm.

At last she found them. Bramble and Heather, Windswept and
Lichen, Snowball, Crag, Twilight and Tundra.

Teeka took a deep breath and shouted out, "Let's go! Move, move, move!"

The reindeer were bewildered by Teeka's voice. Their heads went up to see who this loud creature was.

But they let her herd them together and headed back toward Winterfarm. Tundra gave her the most trouble. Teeka didn't know that he considered himself the leader and was not used to being bossed around. He liked to stay next to Twilight, but she was separated from him and running near the front. When they got to the barn, Teeka put them in different stalls. Tundra snorted impatiently.

By the next morning when Teeka went into the barn, all the reindeer were restless and upset. Lichen was frightened of Crag who kept nipping at him.

Bramble was so worried, she drove Heather wild. And Twilight kept calling out to Tundra who was just plain angry and stamping his hooves.

Teeka groomed each reindeer. She wanted them to look sleek and glossy for Santa. One by one, she brushed and combed their coats and pushed and pulled at their tangled manes. She brushed so long and hard that their ears started to turn pink.

Teeka took the reindeer outside. Now she was ready for the real training to begin. Snowflakes danced in the air as she tried to stand them in two lines and put on their harnesses. But they wouldn't stay lined up. She had put Tundra at the back with Heather instead of at the front with Twilight, so he kicked out at Heather who then bolted into Bramble.

Teeka scolded the reindeer. "Don't move!" she cried. But they all ran off wild-eyed, and she had to go after them and bring them back.

The next day Teeka harnessed the reindeer in the barn before taking them out into the snow. Everything went right until she got them lined up outside and tried to steer them first to the left and then to the right. To make the sleigh fly, they would need to pull together smoothly. But everything went wrong.

Tundra crashed into Heather, Snowball blew up at Bramble. Windswept knocked over Twilight. And then, Lichen locked antlers with Crag.

"Stop!" Teeka cried, as she watched the reindeer paw the air.
"Unhook!" she shouted, as they tried to free their long antlers.

Then Lichen and Crag fell over into the snow. The harder they pulled, the more their antlers locked. The reindeer were frantic and Teeka only made it worse by yelling at them.

Tundra and Heather rushed to help, but the antlers did not break free. Windswept nudged at Lichen, and Bramble ran to help Crag. But the more they tried to help, the more they got tangled up themselves. Their necks strained and their muscles bulged, but their antlers did not budge.

Teeka wailed, "Oh, please! It's almost Christmas Eve!"

But the reindeer could not move.

A frosty silence hung in the air.

DEC 16